A Fall Alphabet Book

F IS FOR FALL

Find our books at Amazon, Barnes & Nobles, Walmart, Books-A-Million, Target, IngramSpark, Kobo, Lulu and more!

Like, Share and Follow us on Facebook, Instagram, TikTok, Threads, Pinterest, YouTube, LinkedIn and more!

www.SlothDreamBooks.com

Text copyright © 2022 by KeriAnne N. Jelinek
Picture copyright © 2022 by KeriAnne N. Jelinek
Pictures Licensed to Sloth Dreams Books & Publishing, LLC.
Published by Sloth Dreams Books & Publishing, LLC.
All Rights Reserved

Sloth Dreams Books & Publishing and colophon are registered trademarks of Sloth Dreams Books & Publishing Co. Ltd.

Sloth Dreams Books for Children
An imprint of Sloth Dreams Books & Publishing, LLC.
Du Bois, PA, 15801

ISBN: 978-7-0462-9261-3

Except in the United States of America, this book is sold subject to the condition that it shall not, by way of trade or otherwise, be lent, re-sold, hired out, or otherwise circulated without the publisher's prior consent in any form of binding or cover other that in which it is published and without a similar condition including this condition being imposed on the subsequent purchaser.

A Fall Alphabet Book
F IS FOR FALL.
Written & Illustrated
by KeriAnne Jelinek

A is for
Apple
Picking.

Juicy ripe apples are ready
for picking in the fall.

A warm crackling bonfire is a fun way to enjoy the cool fall evenings.

C is for Cider.
Drinking fresh apple cider
is a delicious way to enjoy
a nice fall day.

APPLE
CIDER

D is for Donuts.
Apple Cider donuts are a scrumptious treat on any fall day.

E is for Equinox.

The Autumn Equinox, September 22, marks the first day of the fall or autumn season.

F is for Fall Festival.

Going to a fall festival is so much fun. You can enjoy yummy food, fall activities, and entertainment.

G is for Gourd.

Gourds are fruit that have hard outer shells. There are many different kinds of gourds. Some are smooth, bumpy, warty and everything in between.

H is for Hayride.

Going on a hayride to the pumpkin patch is a fun way to celebrate the fall harvest and life on the farm.

I is for Indian Corn.
Indian Corn is a multi-colored corn that ripens during the summer and is ready to be harvested in the fall.

J is for Jacket.

A jacket will keep you warm outside on
a cool and crisp fall day.

R is for Kettle Corn

Kettle Corn is a yummy, sweet treat you can eat on a fun day out at the Fall Festival.

L is for Leaves.
A pile of colorful fall leaves is fun to jump in on a sunny fall day.

M is for Moon.

The full harvest moon shines brightly on a beautiful fall night.

N is for Nut.
Acorns are a kind of nut that many animals eat during the fall.

O is for October.

October is the tenth month of the year and is celebrated as the start of the fall season.

October

P is for Pumpkin.

Pumpkin is a fruit that has a hard shell. Pumpkins are used for carving, baking, cooking and decorating during the fall season.

WILLOW VIEW
Farm Co.
EST. 1960

Q is for Quilt.

A quilt is a traditional blanket made out of fabric squares sewn together to make a thick blanket.

The fall season has many rainy days. It often rains during the fall as it transitions from hot weather into cold weather.

S is for sweater.

Wearing a thick sweater on a cold fall day can make you feel warm and cozy.

T is for Tree.

Trees start to drop their dazzling colored leaves in the fall. Trees are a beautiful part of the fall season.

U is for
Umbrella.
Umbrellas are great to have
handy for those fall rainy days.

V is for Vibrant.
Chrysanthemums are vibrant, bright-colored flowers that are in full bloom in the fall. They come in all colors of the rainbow.

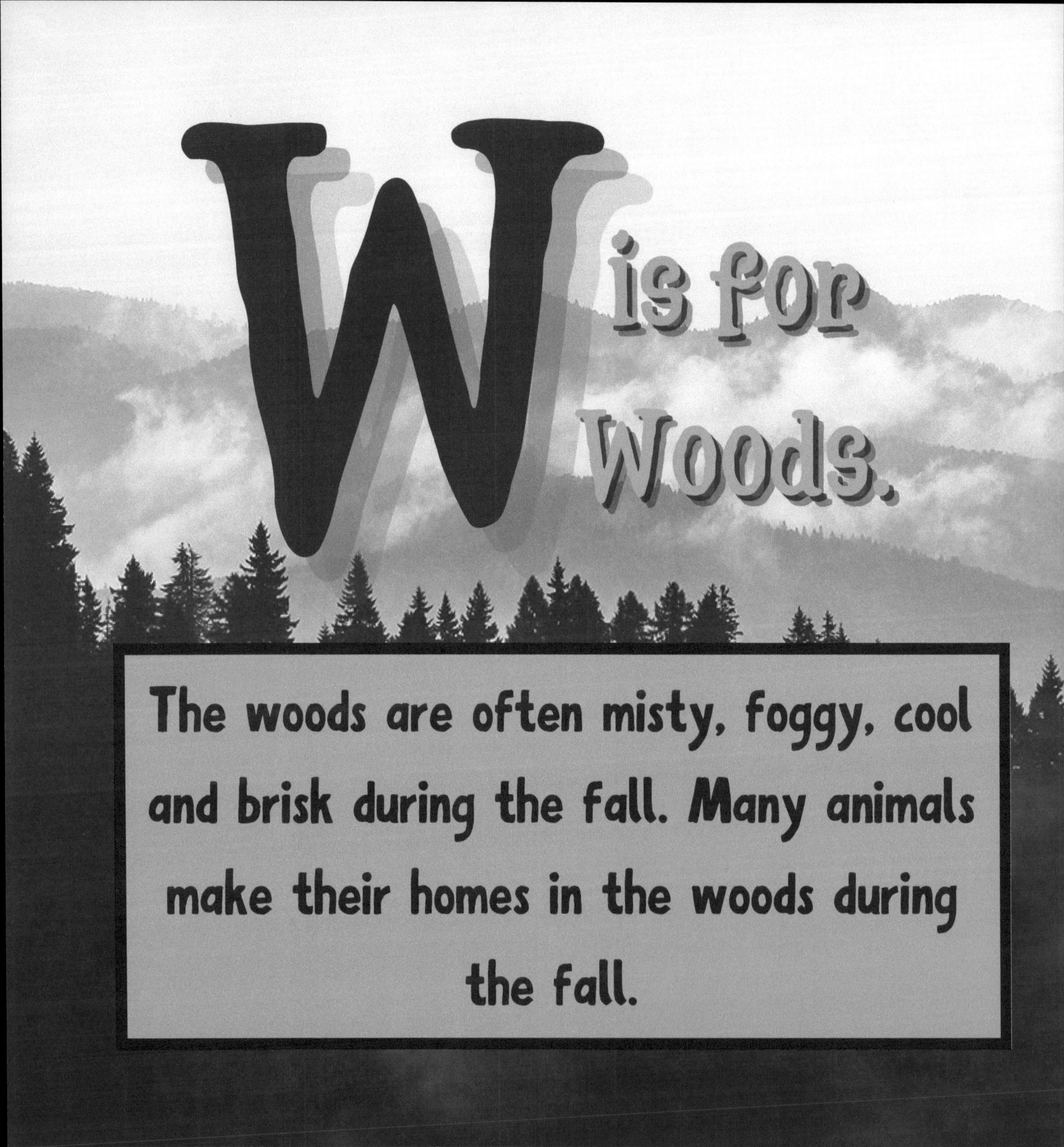

W is for Woods.

The woods are often misty, foggy, cool and brisk during the fall. Many animals make their homes in the woods during the fall.

Pumpkin bread is an eXcellent treat in the fall. It is yummy, sweet and is a very tasty snack on a cool fall day.

Y is for Yellow.

Yellow leaves are extremely beautiful to see in the fall. Aspen leaves are bright yellow when they change colors in the fall.

Z is for maZe.
A corn maZe is a really fun fall activity to do with your family and friends.

CORN MAZE

Happy
Fall Y'all

www.ingramcontent.com/pod-product-compliance
Lightning Source LLC
LaVergne TN
LVHW071621180726
843512LV00002B/218